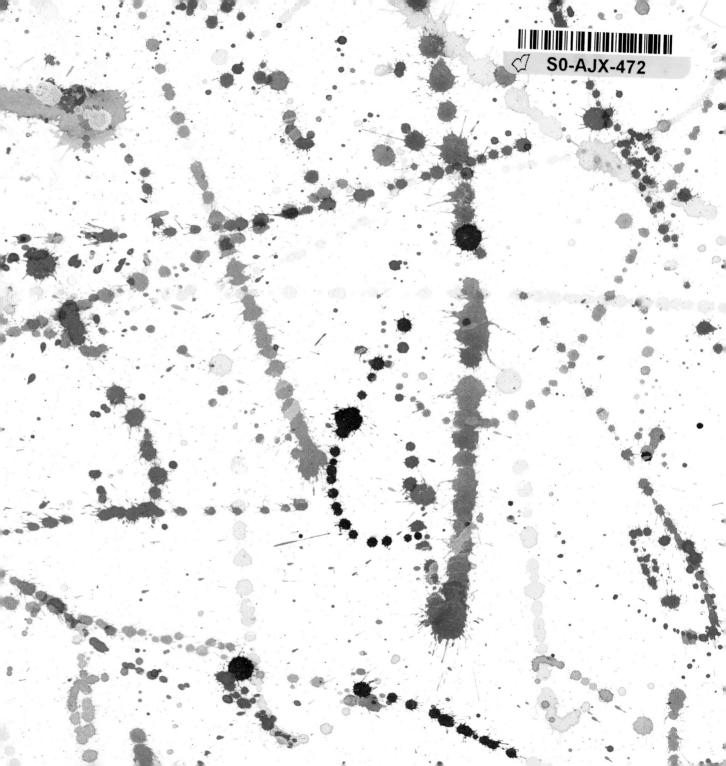

Paint Me!

Written and illustrated
by Sarah Frances Hardy

Sky Pony Press
New York

For my mom . . .
who cleaned up lots of spilled paint.

Sky Pony Press books may be purchased in bulk at special discounts for sales promotion, corporate gifts, fund-raising, or education-al purposes. Special editions can also be created to specifications. For details, contact the Special Sales Department, Sky Pony Press, 307 West 36th Street, 11th Floor, New York, NY 10018 or info@skyhorsepublishing.com.

Sky Pony® is a registered trademark of Skyhorse Publishing, Inc.®, a Delaware corporation.

Visit our website at www.skyponypress.com.

10 9 8 7 6 5 4 3 2 1

Manufactured in China, January 2014
This product conforms to CPSIA 2008

Library of Congress Cataloging-in-Publication Data

Hardy, Sarah Frances, author, illustrator.
Paint me! / written and illustrated by Sarah Frances Hardy.
pages cm
Summary: "A little girl discovers all colors of paint before needing a bath in this colorful book"– Provided by publisher.
ISBN 978-1-62873-813-1 (hardback)
[1. Color–Fiction. 2. Painting–Fiction.] I. Title.
PZ7.H221447Pai 2014
[E]–dc23
2013037352

Pink me.

Purple me.

Orange me.

Green me.

Yellow
me.

Pink me
some more!

Gray me.

Sky blue me.

Ra nbow me!

Dry me.

Pajama me.

Tuck me.

Sleep me.

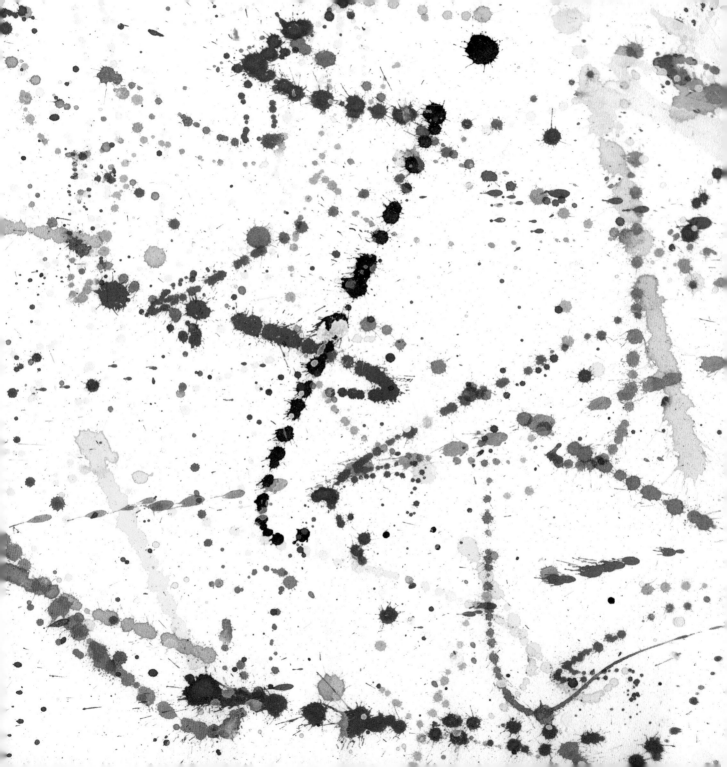